EVERETT ANDERSON'S YEAR

EVERETT

ANDERSON'S YEAR

BY LUCILLE CLIFTON

ILLUSTRATED BY ANN GRIFALCONI

HOLT, RINEHART AND WINSTON
New York • Chicago • San Francisco

Printed in the United States of America
10 9 8 7 6 5 4 3 2

Library of Congress Cataloging in Publication Data

Clifton, Lucille, 1936-
    Everett Anderson's year.
    SUMMARY: A poem for each month of the year reflects
the major and minor events in the life of a young boy.
    [1. Family life—Poetry.   2. Seasons—Poetry]
I. Grifalconi, Ann, illus.   II. Title.
PZ8.3.C573Ex   811′.5′4   73-22424
ISBN 0-03-012736-X

Designer: Ann Grifalconi

-14817-

JANUARY

"Walk tall in the world,"
says Mama
to Everett Anderson.
"The year is new and
so are the days,
walk tall in the world,"
she says.

FEBRUARY

Everett Anderson
in the snow
is a specially
ice cream boy to know
as he jumps and calls
and spins and falls
with his chocolate nose and
vanilla toes.

MARCH

What if a wind
would blow a boy
away,
where would he go
to play?
What if a wind
would blow him back
next day,
what would his
Mama say?
This time instead of
run outside
Everett Anderson thinks
he'll hide.

APRIL

Rain is good
for washing leaves
and stones and bricks and
even eyes,
and if you hold
your head just so
you can almost see
the tops of skies.

MAY

Remember the time we took a ride
to the country and saw a horse and a cow,
and remember the time I picked a weed
and Daddy laughed and laughed real loud,
and remember he spanked me for throwing stones?
I wish it could be like that now,
thinks Everett Anderson when he's alone.

JUNE

In 14A, till Mama comes home
bells are for ringing
and windows for singing
and halls are for skating
and doors are for waiting.

JULY

Everett Anderson thinks he'll make
America a birthday cake
only the sugar is almost gone
and payday's not till later on.

AUGUST

Now I am seven Mama can stay
from work and play with me all day.
I'll teach her marbles and rope and ball
and let her win sometimes, and all
our friends will be calling each other and saying
Everett Anderson's Mama and him are playing.

SEPTEMBER

I already know where Africa is
and I already know how to
count to ten and
I went to school every day last year,
why do I have to go again?

OCTOBER

Don't run when you see
this terrible monster
with a horrible nose and
awful eyes,
under those jaggedy
monstery teeth
it's Everett Anderson
in disguise!

NOVEMBER

Thank you for the things we have,
thank you for Mama and turkey and fun,
thank you for Daddy wherever he is,
thank you for me, Everett Anderson.

DECEMBER

"The end of a thing
is never the end,
something is always
being born like
a year or a baby."

"I don't understand,"
Everett Anderson says.
"I don't understand where
the whole thing's at."

"It's just about Love,"
his Mama smiles.
"It's all about Love and
you know about that."

ABOUT THE AUTHOR

Lucille Clifton is the award-winning author of *Some of the Days of Everett Anderson, Everett Anderson's Christmas Coming, All Us Come Cross the Water*, and *The Times They Used to Be*. These and her other works continue to win her wide acclaim. She and her husband live with their six children in Baltimore, Maryland. When she does have free time, she enjoys acting, reading, and people-watching.

ABOUT THE ARTIST

Ann Grifalconi, a city child herself, spent her seasons of the year roaming through the parks and exciting streets of New York City. Some of her memories became the ever-popular picture book *City Rhythms*. She has written and illustrated several books, including *The Toy Trumpet* and *The Matter With Lucy*. As an illustrator, she has collaborated with many writers in over thirty books.

ABOUT THE BOOK

The text of *Everett Anderson's Year* is set in Times Roman with display in Albertus. Ms. Grifalconi has used woodcut printed in line. The book is printed by offset.

82140

811
CL

Clifton, Lucille

Everett Anderson's
year

DATE			